Maze of Hearts

Ulrich Germania

Imprint

Book title:
Maze of Hearts

Subtitle:
Two Love Stories Set in a Mirror Maze

Series:
Romantic Encounters at the Funfair

AI Note:
AI generated story, initiated and revised by the author
Translated from German into American English by an AI.

Author:
Ulrich Germania © 2025

Publisher:
BoD · Books on Demand GmbH
Überseering 33, 22297 Hamburg, bod@bod.de

Print:
Libri Plureos GmbH
Friedensallee 273, 22763 Hamburg

ISBN: 978-3-8192-6688-1

Contents

Picture credits:

The images on the book cover and the illustrations in the book were generated by AI and modified using programs for photo manipulation.

AI Note:

Author Ulrich Germania came up with the characters and the plot, the AI wrote the stories, then they were revised and improved by the author.
The translation from German into American English was also done by an AI.
Proofreading: The translation was checked and improved by another AI.

Contact:

Ulrich.Germania@online.de

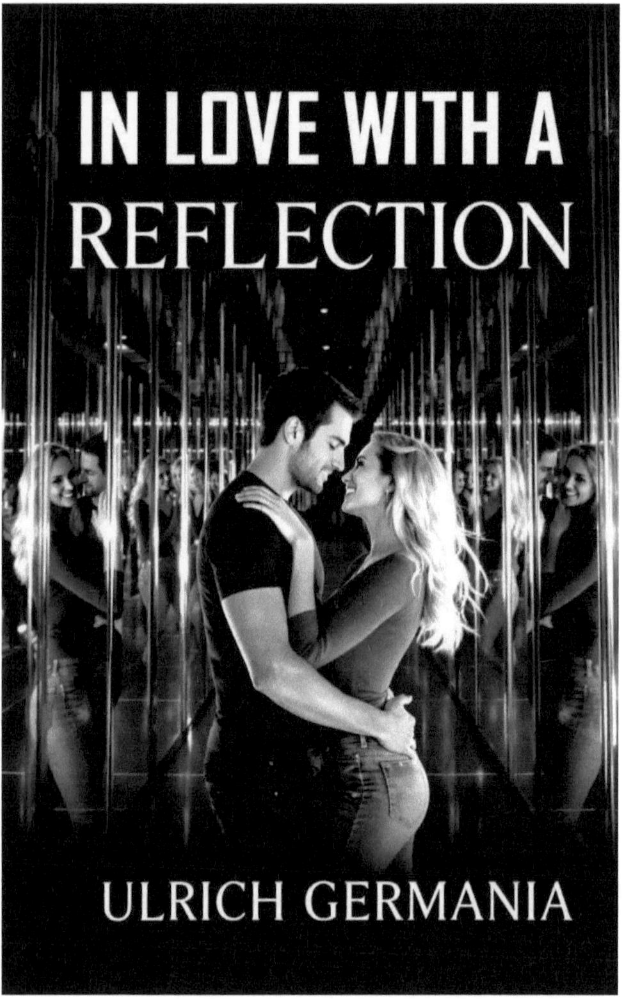
IN LOVE WITH A
REFLECTION
ULRICH GERMANIA

The Labyrinth of Mirrors

The fairground shimmered with lights, laughter, and tantalizing aromas. Cotton candy, roasted almonds, and deep-fried treats tempted visitors at every turn. The rattle of rollercoasters blended with joyful screams and the delighted squeals of children. But amid all this hustle and bustle, one attraction stood out—not for its noise, but for its quiet allure: the mirror maze.

From the outside, it seemed unremarkable—just a large tent with ornate, glowing letters spelling out: *Magical Labyrinth of Mirrors*.

An old showman with a twirled mustache stood in front, calling out in a deep voice, "Enter if you dare—and see if you can find your way back out!" The twinkle in his eye promised that it wouldn't be easy.

Inside, a world of mirrors awaited—angled, doubled, multiplied. Some reflections stretched into infinite chains; others were so perfect it was impossible to tell wall from passage. Nothing was as it seemed.

Within minutes, visitors lost all sense of direction—and of time. The mirrors played tricks with light and perspective, turning every step into a puzzle.

The mirror labyrinth became a test of will, perception, and patience. Some stumbled out eventually, laughing in relief. Others gave up and had to be led out. But for most, it was a thrilling adventure — a game between illusion and reality. And that's exactly what drew them in.

The Wandering Visitors

That evening, several groups ventured inside. Ten people entered—five women, five men—completely unaware of the maze's tricks.

A couple clung tightly to each other.

“Don’t let go!” the young woman squealed as her boyfriend briefly released her hand. They laughed, spinning around in love and confusion. Every turn confronted them with multiplied versions of themselves.

A middle-aged man tried to outsmart the maze with logic.
“If I go this way… no, that’s a reflection… maybe here?” He scratched his head and hesitated again.

Nearby, a group of young girls giggled their way through the corridors.

“I see myself *everywhere*!” one shouted. “How many of me are there?”

Their laughter echoed through the maze as they made faces in the glass.

Meanwhile, a confident voice called out: "This way! I've found the exit!"—only to slam into a mirrored wall.

Thud. "Oof!" Laughter followed.

Everyone in the labyrinth experienced their own little adventure. Some got lost. Some found each other. Some quite literally came face-to-face with themselves.

Carlos and Rosa in the Maze

Carlos strolled through the fairground. He lived nearby and just wanted to see if anything had changed this year.

Nothing new caught his eye. The usual rides. The same sweet smells. He wasn't hungry. But then he saw the mirror maze. He'd never tried one before.

"Why not?" he murmured, stepping inside.

Immediately, the maze surrounded him in shimmering reflections. Left? Right? Straight? He had no clue. The mirrors distorted his image, tricking him into thinking he wasn't alone—or that he was looking at someone else entirely.

Then, suddenly, he stopped.

A girl appeared in the mirror—long blonde hair, a short denim skirt, and a bright red top that sparkled in the light. Her eyes met his, and Carlos felt his heartbeat quicken.

He waved. She waved back.

And then she was gone.

The maze began to play with him. He caught glimpses of her—but they were just reflections. Sometimes, she seemed to be standing right in front of him... but it was only a reflection of a reflection.

Still, they knew of each other. Every so often, they managed a wave, a shy smile. A playful game of hide-and-seek began—between illusion and reality. And Carlos knew: he had to find her.

Carlos Meets Marisa

Carlos wandered deeper, heart pounding. But instead of the blonde girl, another woman suddenly stood in front of him—this time, unmistakably real.

"Hey, you're looking for Rosa, right?" she said with a grin. "She's the one with the red top."

Carlos blinked. "Her name's Rosa? How do you know I'm looking for her?"

"I'm Marisa, her best friend. I saw you chasing her reflection through the mirrors."

Carlos laughed awkwardly. "I'm Carlos. And yeah... I think it was love at first sight. Any idea where she went?"

Marisa shrugged. "No clue—I lost her too. But wow, you fell for her *reflection*?"

Carlos sighed. "Apparently, I did."

Marisa laughed.

“Oh man, that’s brilliant. Alright, Romeo, we’ll look for her together. You go that way, I’ll go this way. Whoever finds her first grabs her hand and doesn’t let go!”

Carlos grinned. “If we make it out of here, drinks are on me—for both of you.”

“It’s a deal!” she said.

They high-fived and split up in search of Rosa.

Marisa Finds Rosa

Marisa pushed through the glittering maze, and suddenly —*bam!*— ran right into Rosa.

"There you are!" she exclaimed, grabbing her friend's hand. "I found the guy you waved to. His name's Carlos — and guess what? He's totally smitten with your reflection."

Rosa burst out laughing. "No way! That's crazy! We have to find him!"

Together, they navigated the mirrored halls, catching occasional glimpses of Carlos—but getting to him was another story.

The Girls Find Carlos

Rosa and Marisa moved more carefully this time, no longer fooled by the reflections. They had a plan.

“Carlos!” Rosa called out. Her voice echoed through the maze. “Where are you?”

“Carlos! Say something!” Marisa added.

At first, nothing but their own echoes answered—until finally, a faint voice:

“I’m here!”

“Again!” Marisa yelled.

“Over here! Can you hear me?”

His voice grew clearer. Was it to the right? Behind them?

Rosa frowned. “He’s close... but these mirrors are so confusing.”

“Forget the mirrors,” Marisa said. “Just follow the voice!”

Step by step, they moved with purpose. Turn left. Sharp right. Past a wall of endless reflections...

And then — there he was.

They froze. Was it really him? Or just another trick?

Carlos stepped forward—and Rosa rushed into his arms.

"There you are!" she gasped, breathless and smiling. She could feel his heart pounding just like hers.

Carlos laughed, the tension melting away. He pulled Marisa into the hug. "I thought I'd never get out."

Marisa chuckled. "Well, now you've found us, and we've found you. Now... you owe us that drink."

Carlos grinned. "I'm a man of my word. Let's go before these mirrors change their minds!"

Hand in hand, they finally found the exit—laughing, relieved, and just a little in love.

At the Beer Garden

Outside, the fresh air felt like a blessing after the dizzying maze. Still buzzing, the trio made their way to the beer garden, where music, laughter, and clinking glasses filled the air.

Carlos ordered drinks, and they found a table. Just as they began to relax, a young man appeared—tall, confident, with a charming grin.

"Carlos! You, with such lovely company?"

Carlos laughed. "Pedro! My friend, meet Rosa and Marisa." He gestured. "I fell in love with her reflection,"—pointing to Rosa—"and she,"—to Marisa—"saved me from losing my mind."

Pedro raised an eyebrow and smiled at Marisa. "May I sit down—or do I have to brave the mirror maze first?"

Marisa laughed. "You'd get hopelessly lost. Just sit—if you're brave enough to fall for me directly, not my reflection."

Pedro chuckled, pulling up a chair.

"That's a risk I'm willing to take."

Everyone laughed, and Carlos raised his glass.

"To reflections, to mazes—and to what's real."

Glasses clinked. Music played. And by the end of the night, two couples had fallen in love—already planning to explore the fairground together again the next day.

ENCHANTING
REFLECTIONS
ULRICH GERMANIA

Enchanting Reflections

Chapter 1:

A Labyrinth Full of Surprises

The old funfair opened only once a year — and only for a single night. It was a place steeped in nostalgia and mystery. The lights of the carousels sparkled like stars, and the air was thick with the scent of cotton candy and roasted almonds. But the heart of the fair wasn't the rollercoaster or the Ferris wheel — it was the legendary mirror maze.

Emma, a young artist with a flair for chaos, stood in front of the entrance and eyed the sign skeptically:

"Magic mirror labyrinth — Come in if you dare!"

"Come in if you dare?" she read aloud with amusement. "Sounds dramatic. But hey, I love drama."

She shrugged and stepped into the maze.

Inside, it was even stranger than she'd imagined. The mirrors were arranged so cleverly that it was nearly impossible to tell if you were headed toward an exit or straight into a wall.

Emma laughed nervously as she saw her reflection multiply endlessly.

"Okay, that's creepy. But also kind of cool."

Meanwhile, Luca, a scientist with a love for order and logic, entered the maze from the opposite side. He had heard rumors that the labyrinth was cursed and was determined to scientifically debunk the myth.

"A curse? Ridiculous," he muttered, pulling out a small notepad to take notes. "It's just tricks with light and mirrors."

But the labyrinth had other plans.

Emma wandered through the corridors, talking to the mirrors as though they could hear her.

"All right, you there," she said to one mirror that reflected her at an odd angle. "Are you the way out or just another mean trick?"

Suddenly, she heard a voice from another corridor.

"Uh, hello? Is anyone there?"

Emma turned and spotted a man looking through the mirrors at her. He had dark hair, glasses, and the unmistakable look of someone thoroughly lost in a maze.

"Oh, hi!" she called out. "Are you lost too?"

"Lost? No, no," Luca replied quickly. "I'm... uh... just studying the structure of the labyrinth."

Emma raised an eyebrow.

"Studying? You mean you're lost and too proud to admit it?"

"What? No!" Luca cleared his throat. "I'm a scientist. I study things. That's my job."

"I see," Emma said with a grin. "And how's that working out for you? Have you figured out the way out yet?"

"Well... not yet," Luca admitted reluctantly. "But I'm working on it."

Emma laughed. "Well, good luck with that, Mr. Scientist. I hope you find the exit before this place drives you mad."

"It won't," Luca said confidently. "I'm immune to stuff like this."

"Oh really?" Emma leaned against a mirror, arms crossed. "Then enjoy your... research."

As they continued to wander, the mirrors began to weave their magic.

Emma kept seeing Luca appear in the mirrors, even when he wasn't around. And Luca noticed that Emma seemed to be smiling at him from the reflections, even though she was actually in a different corridor.

“That's ridiculous,” Luca muttered as he caught himself smiling back. "It's just a trick. It can't be real."

But the longer they were in the labyrinth, the more they began to embrace the strange connection the mirrors created between them.

And although they didn't know it, this was just the beginning of a completely crazy, magical and incredibly romantic night.

Chapter 2:

Mirror, Mirror on the Wall

Emma and Luca kept walking, still on different sides of the maze, yet somehow connected by the enchanted mirrors.

Emma started to enjoy the strange setup. It amused her how Luca tried to approach everything logically, even while his reflection kept popping up unexpectedly.

“So, Mr. Scientist,” Emma called through the mirrored halls, “still analyzing your precious maze?”

“I’m not analyzing the mirrors,” Luca replied, trying to stay serious. “I’m studying the structure of the labyrinth.”

“Uh-huh,” Emma grinned. “And how’s that going? Any explanation yet for why you keep showing up in the mirrors I look into?”

“It’s just an optical effect,” Luca explained. “The mirrors are placed in such a way that they create recurring reflections that—”

"Yeah, yeah, yeah," Emma interrupted. "I know how mirrors work. But that still doesn't explain why *you* keep turning up. Maybe the maze just has a thing for you."

"The maze has a thing for me?" Luca frowned. "That's ridiculous."

"Well, maybe it likes me too," Emma said with a mischievous smile. "Or maybe it likes us *together*. Who knows?"

Luca shook his head. "That's absurd. Mirrors don't have feelings."

"Maybe not," Emma replied. "But they can show you what you *really* want. And maybe the labyrinth wants us to get to know each other."

"That's just..." Luca searched for the right words. "That's completely irrational."

"Exactly," Emma said brightly. "But also kind of romantic, don't you think?"

Luca sighed. "I'm a scientist. Romance isn't really my thing."

"Oh, that's a shame," Emma said. "Because romance *is* my thing. And I think you should give it a try."

"Give it a try?" Luca frowned. "How would I even do that?"

"Well, you could start by giving me a compliment," Emma suggested.

"A compliment?" Luca thought for a moment. "Well, uh... you have a very... interesting laugh."

Emma laughed again. "Interesting laugh? That's the weirdest compliment I've ever gotten."

"Well, I *am* a scientist," Luca said sheepishly. "I'm not exactly smooth."

"I can tell," Emma teased. "But honestly? That kind of makes it better."

Chapter 3:

The Magic of Mirrors

As they continued through the labyrinth, the magic of the mirrors grew stronger. They began to reflect not just themselves — but vivid glimpses of a possible future together.

Emma saw herself and Luca having a picnic in the park, laughing as if nothing else in the world mattered. Luca saw them sharing a candlelit dinner, gazing into each other's eyes as time seemed to stop.

"This is insane," Luca muttered, staring at the scenes. "It can't be real."

"Maybe it's not," Emma said. "But it *feels* real. Isn't that what matters?"

"I don't know," Luca said hesitantly. "I'm a man of facts, not feelings."

“Well, maybe it’s time you started believing in feelings,” Emma said. “Because feelings are what make life worth living.”

“That’s just...” Luca struggled again.

“Whatever it is,” Emma said softly, “it’s beautiful. Don’t you think?”

Luca sighed. “Maybe you’re right. Maybe I really should start believing in feelings.”

“That’s the spirit,” Emma said with a grin. “And you know what? I think the labyrinth really does like us.”

“Yeah, maybe it does,” Luca replied, smiling. “Maybe it really does.”

Chapter 4:

The Exit

After what felt like an eternity, Emma and Luca finally found the exit. They stepped out into the cool night air and took a deep breath.

"Wow," Emma said. "That was... intense."

"Yeah, it was," Luca agreed. "But it was also... beautiful."

"Beautiful?" Emma raised an eyebrow. "That's the first time I've heard you use that word. Are you sure you're still a scientist?"

"Positive," Luca said with a smile. "But maybe I'm also a bit of a romantic."

"I like that," Emma said. "Maybe we should come back sometime. You know, just to make sure it really *was* magical."

"Yeah, maybe we should," Luca said.

“But next time — no notepad.” Emma demanded.

“It’s a deal. No notepad.” Luca promised.

And so, their night in the mirror maze ended with a smile, a promise, and the quiet certainty that the magic of love often waits in the most unexpected places.

Chapter 5:

The Magic of Everyday Life

Something had changed that night. Emma and Luca had only met hours earlier, but it already felt as though they'd always been part of each other's lives.

After leaving the maze, they wandered through the rest of the fair together. The lights, the sounds, the smells — everything seemed more vivid, more alive.

"You know what I'm thinking right now?" Emma asked as they passed a stand selling cotton candy. "That we might never have met if it weren't for the maze."

"You're right," Luca said, smiling. "And I'm glad we did — in *that* maze."

"Me too," Emma said, reaching for his hand. "And... I think the labyrinth not only introduced us to each other, but also showed us what we want."

"That's an interesting theory," Luca said. "But I'm still a scientist. I need proof."

"Proof?" Emma laughed. "All right, then let's prove it. How about we meet again tomorrow? No magic, no mirrors — just the two of us."

"Sounds like a solid plan," Luca said. "But where?"

"How about the park by the old oak tree?" Emma suggested. "It's quiet there."

"Perfect," Luca nodded. "I'll meet you there at three o'clock."

"It's a deal," Emma said with a grin. "And come without your notepad."

"Without a notepad," Luca promised, chuckling.

Chapter 6:

A Date in the Park

The next day was warm and sunny — perfect for a picnic. Emma wore a light summer dress and carried a small picnic basket.

Luca, punctual as ever, was already waiting beneath the old oak tree. He had laid out a blanket and brought a few books with him.

"Wow, you really thought of everything," Emma said as she sat down. "Blanket, books, even wine?"

"Well," Luca replied, smiling, "I figured we could use a little romance. Plus, I read that picnics are considered romantic."

"You read that, huh?" Emma laughed. "Well, I hope you packed something to eat, too."

"Of course," he said, opening the basket. "Sandwiches, fruit... even some macarons."

Emma blinked. "Okay, now I'm impressed. You're a full-on romantic."

"I learn quickly," Luca said, giving her a wink.

As they ate and talked, it became clear that the magic of the mirror maze hadn't stayed behind. It had followed them. They laughed about the absurdity of it all, shared dreams and fears, and found themselves slowly unfolding into each other.

"You know what I wish?" Emma asked, leaning back and gazing at the sky. "That we'll always be this happy."

"I wish that too," Luca said, taking her hand. "And I believe we will be."

"That's sweet," Emma said, smiling. "You know what else I've been thinking?"

"What?"

"Maybe the maze wasn't a curse after all," she said. "Maybe it was a blessing."

"Yeah," Luca said, smiling softly. "A blessing that brought us together."

Chapter 7:

A New Beginning

The days passed, and Emma and Luca grew closer with each one. They explored the city, went to the movies, visited museums, and simply enjoyed being together.

The magic of the mirror maze seemed to linger — not in the form of illusions or reflections, but in the way they looked at the world now. Everything felt fuller. Brighter.

"You know what I'm thinking?" Emma said one evening as they curled up on the sofa watching a movie. "Maybe we should go back to the maze sometime."

"Really?" Luca asked, surprised. "Why?"

"Just to see if the magic is still there," she said. "Or maybe just to remind us how it all started."

"That sounds like a great idea," Luca said.

"But without the notepad," Emma demanded.

"Without the notepad," Luca confirmed, laughing.

"Just the two of us — and the magic." Emma said, resting her head on his shoulder.

Chapter 8:

The Magic Remains

A year later, on the anniversary of their first meeting, Emma and Luca stood once more before the mirror maze. Hand in hand, they stepped inside, letting the shimmering reflections surround them again.

"You know what I'm thinking right now?" Emma asked as they wandered through the glowing corridors. "We may never really know if the maze is truly magical — or if it was just *our* magic."

"Maybe it's both," Luca said. "Maybe the magic of the maze is the magic we carry inside us."

"That's beautiful," Emma said with a smile. "And… I think we'll carry that magic with us — always."

"Yes," Luca said, kissing her gently. "Forever."

And so, their story ended where it began — in a labyrinth of mirrors — with a smile, a kiss, and the quiet certainty that the magic of love would always be with them.

More books by Ulrich Germania

If you enjoyed these two romantic fairground stories, then you are sure to enjoy other short stories that Ulrich Germania has come up with.

Many stories by the author tell of romantic encounters in unusual places.

AI-Note: For the following stories applies: Ulrich Germania came up with the characters and the plot, the AI wrote the story, and then the author revised and improved it.

Fair of Hearts
Short, heartwarming fairground story

Doctors at the funfair
Not a doctor's story, but somehow.

The Goddess of Love at the Fair
A fair with a mystical flair

In Love with Costumes
Romantic encounters at a cosplay event

Not supported by AI:
First Revenge, then the Bride
Wild west story with showdown and love at first sight.

Book Series

Romantic Encounters at the Funfair